little Miss Chatterbox

by Roger Hargreaves

Little Miss Chatterbox talked more than a lot.

She talked all the time.

Day in and day out, week after week, month after month, year in and year out!

She never stopped!

She didn't know it, but she even talked in her sleep!

She had a brother.

I bet you can guess what his name was!

Can't you?

That's right!

Mr Chatterbox!

She looks a bit like him, don't you think?

You should have heard them when they got together!

You couldn't get a word in edgeways.

Or sideways.

Or anyways!

Have you ever heard about somebody
being able to talk the hind leg off a donkey?

Well, Mr Chatterbox could talk both hind
legs off a donkey.

And his sister could talk the hind leg
off an elephant!

Now, this story is about the time Little
Miss Chatterbox decided to get herself a job.

Which she did.

In a bank.

In Happyland.

At ten o'clock one Monday morning
Mr Happy strolled into the
HappyToLendYou Bank in the middle
of Happytown.

He took out his cheque book, wrote
a cheque, and went to the counter.

Behind the counter, on her first morning
at work, stood Little Miss Chatterbox.

She smiled at Mr Happy.

Mr Happy smiled back.

"Good morning," he said, cheerfully.

"Well," said Little Miss Chatterbox,
taking a deep breath ...

"For the time of year it is a good morning but not as good as the morning we had yesterday and I dare say tomorrow morning will be an even better morning but it's quite a good morning for Monday morning and..."

And she went on and on and on until it was time for the bank to shut.

Mr Happy was still standing there, with his mouth open in amazement.

He'd been there for hours!

"And now," continued Little Miss Chatterbox, "it'stimeforthebanktoshutand timeformetogohomesogoodbyeand nicetalkingtoyouand..."

And she went home, leaving poor Mr Happy without any money.

The following morning she was fired!

She got herself another job.

In a restaurant.

The Eatalot!

It was Tuesday morning, and at midday Mr Greedy walked into the restaurant and sat himself down at his usual corner table.

He always ate there on Tuesdays because that was the day they served extra large portions.

The waitress came up to take his order.

"What's the soup of the day?" Mr Greedy asked the waitress.

"Well," said Little Miss Chatterbox, for she was the waitress. "Thesoupofthedayis tomatobutwealsohaveothersoupsonthe menusuchasoxtailandvegetableand chickennoodlebutwehavelots ofotherthingstostartwithsuchas..."

And she went on and on and on.

Until midnight!

Mr Greedy still sitting there, listening, in amazement.

He'd been there for twelve hours!

Listening!

"And now," continued Little Miss Chatterbox, "it's time for the Eatalot Restaurant to shut and for me to go home so goodbye and nice talking to you and..."

And she went home, leaving poor Mr Greedy feeling rather empty.

The next morning she was fired!

The same thing happened all week long.

On Thursday morning she was fired from her job as an assistant in a hat shop.

Miss Splendid went into the shop to buy herself a new hat, but she couldn't!

"Oh Madam I've just the hat for you and I know you're going to love it because it's pink and pink is your colour and it..."

It was all talk, and no hat!

On Friday morning she was fired from her job as a secretary to Mr Uppity.

Mr Uppity, incidentally, was the richest man in the world!

I just thought you'd like to know.

But poor Mr Uppity didn't make any money the day that Little Chatterbox was working for him.

Oh no!

"Oh Mr Uppity I've never worked in an office before and isn't it exciting and would you like a cup of coffee and are you as rich as everybody says you are and it..."

It was all talk and no work!

But, this story has a happy ending because at the very end of that week Little Miss Chatterbox managed to find herself a job that suited her down to the ground.

And up to the sky!

That Saturday evening Mr Chatterbox was at home in Chatterbox Cottage.

Which was where he lived.

Mr Chatterbox was cross because his watch had stopped and he had arranged to meet Little Miss Sunshine at seven o'clock and he had no idea what the time was.

So, he decided to telephone the Speaking Clock to find out what time it was.

He dialled the number.

"...at the third stroke it will be six twenty five and fifteen seconds!"

Little Miss Chatterbox took a deep breath.

PIP PIP PIP

"At the third stroke it will be six twenty five and twenty seconds!"

PIP PIP PIP

"That's funny," thought Mr Chatterbox to himself. "That sounds just like my sister!"

CUT ALONG DOTTED LINE AND RETURN THIS WHOLE PAGE

3 Great Offers for MR.MEN Fans!

1 New Mr. Men or Little Miss Library Bus Presentation Cases

A brand new stronger, roomier school bus library box, with sturdy carrying handle and stay-closed fasteners.
The full colour, wipe-clean boxes make a great home for your full collection.
They're just £5.99 inc P&P and free bookmark!

☐ MR. MEN ☐ LITTLE MISS (please tick and order overleaf)

2 Door Hangers and Posters

In every Mr. Men and Little Miss book like this one, you will find a special token. Collect 6 tokens and we will send you a brilliant Mr. Men or Little Miss poster and a Mr. Men or Little Miss double sided full colour bedroom door hanger of your choice. Simply tick your choice in the list and tape a 50p coin for your two items to this page.

Door Hangers (please tick)

☐ Mr. Nosey & Mr. Muddle
☐ Mr. Slow & Mr. Busy
☐ Mr. Messy & Mr. Quiet
☐ Mr. Perfect & Mr. Forgetful
☐ Little Miss Fun & Little Miss Late
☐ Little Miss Helpful & Little Miss Tidy
☐ Little Miss Busy & Little Miss Brainy
☐ Little Miss Star & Little Miss Fun

Posters (please tick)

☐ MR.MEN
☐ LITTLE MISS

PLEASE STICK YOUR 50P COIN HERE

Beautiful Fridge Magnets – any **2** for £**2.00**!
inc.P&P

special collector's items!

our first and second* choices from the list below

racters!

	2nd Choice	
☐ Mr. Daydream	☐ Mr. Happy	☐ Mr. Daydream
☐ Mr. Tickle	☐ Mr. Lazy	☑ Mr. Tickle
☐ Mr. Topsy-Turvy	☐ Mr. Greedy	☐ Mr. Topsy-Turvy	☐ Mr. Greedy
☐ Mr. Bounce	☐ Mr. Funny	☑ Mr. Bounce	☐ Mr. Funny
☐ Mr. Small	☐ Little Miss Giggles	☐ Mr. Bump	☑ Little Miss Giggles
☐ Mr. Snow	☐ Little Miss Splendid	☐ Mr. Small	☑ Little Miss Splendid
☐ Mr. Wrong	☐ Little Miss Naughty	☑ Mr. Snow	☑ Little Miss Naughty
	☐ Little Miss Sunshine	☐ Mr. Wrong	☑ Little Miss Sunshine

*Only in case your first choice is out of stock.

─── TO BE COMPLETED BY AN ADULT ───

**To apply for any of these great offers, ask an adult to complete the coupon below and send it with
the appropriate payment and tokens, if needed, to MR. MEN CLASSIC OFFER, PO BOX 715, HORSHAM RH12 5WG**

☐ Please send ____ Mr. Men Library case(s) and/or ____ Little Miss Library case(s) at £5.99 each inc P&P

☐ Please send a poster and door hanger as selected overleaf. I enclose six tokens plus a 50p coin for P&P

☐ Please send me ____ pair(s) of Mr. Men/Little Miss fridge magnets, as selected above at £2.00 inc P&P

Fan's Name _____

Address _____

_____ **Postcode** _____

Date of Birth _____

Name of Parent/Guardian _____

Total amount enclosed £ _____

☐ **I enclose a cheque/postal order payable to Egmont Books Limited**

☐ **Please charge my MasterCard/Visa/Amex/Switch or Delta account** (delete as appropriate)

| | | | | | | | | | | | | | | | | | | Card Number |

Expiry date __/__ **Signature** _____

Please allow 28 days for delivery. Offer is only available while stocks last. We reserve the right to change the terms
of this offer at any time and we offer a 14 day money back guarantee. This does not affect your statutory rights.
Data Protection Act: If you do not wish to receive other similar offers from us or companies we recommend, please
tick this box ☐. Offers apply to UK only.

MR.MEN   LITTLE MISS
Mr. Men and Little Miss™ & ©Mrs. Roger Hargreaves

CUT ALONG DOTTED LINE AND RETURN THIS WHOLE PAGE